Puffin Books

My Dog Sunday

D0610639

'I'm afraid you are too young,' said the lady firmly, and that was that. Ben had to leave the Dog's Home without any dog at all, not even an imaginary one like Kathy had.

He didn't even look at Kathy, he felt so bad. They just trudged off to the park – Ben, Kathy and little Jimmy and *no* dog – same as always but more miserable because now they had nothing to look forward to.

Later, up in the tree-house, Ben caught sight of a strange, shaggy animal galloping through the trees. From all those dog books he'd had from the library, he knew it was an Old English sheepdog and that it would run about with them and roll and lick them, and do everything that he had always wanted a dog of his own to do. It would even give little Jimmy rides, and in the evening it would come home with him to live . . . It doesn't happen quite like that, but at least some of Ben's dreams come true in this appealing and sensitive story.

Leila Berg

My Dog Sunday

Illustrated by Peter Edwards

Puffin Books

PUFFIN BOOKS

Published by the Penguin Group
Penguin Books Ltd, 27 Wrights Lane, London W8 5TZ, England
Viking Penguin, a division of Penguin Books USA Inc.
375 Hudson Street, New York, New York 10014, USA
Penguin Books Australia Ltd, Ringwood, Victoria, Australia
Penguin Books Canada Ltd, 2801 John Street, Markham, Ontario, Canada L3R 1B4
Penguin Books (NZ) Ltd, 182–190 Wairau Road, Auckland 10, New Zealand

Penguin Books Ltd, Registered Offices: Harmondsworth, Middlesex, England

First published by Hamish Hamilton Children's Books 1968
Published in Puffin Books 1979
19 18 17 16 15 14 13 12 11

Text copyright © Leila Berg, 1968
Illustrations copyright © Peter Edwards, 1979
All rights reserved

Printed in England by Clays Ltd, St Ives plc
Set in Monotype Baskerville

BEN looked sideways at Kathy. She was kicking a ball along beside her. She made it trickle at her side, keeping pace with her. Sometimes she would walk a little quicker, so that it followed her. Sometimes she went more slowly and let the ball go on in front; then, it would roll to a halt at last and wait for her.

Ben knew what Kathy was doing. He had known for a long time. She was pretending the ball was a dog. That was why he had known it was safe to take her to the Dogs' Home with him. He could trust her.

The ball rolled into the gutter. Kathy stood and waited. Ben walked slower. He didn't think Kathy would want him to show he knew the

ball was a dog; but he didn't want to go round the corner, out of her sight.

'What's Kathy doing?' said Jimmy. 'Why isn't she coming?'

'I don't know,' said Ben. 'Anyway, she is coming. She's coming now.'

'Where are we going?' said Jimmy. 'I'm tired. I want a piggyback.'

Ben didn't answer the first question. He picked Jimmy up and sat him on the wall, and from here Jimmy flung his arms joyously round Ben's neck, jumped off the wall and hung from him like a sack. Ben knew he would do this – he always did – but it still made him stagger. 'Sit higher!' he said. 'You're choking me!'

They jogged a little way along the dusty pavement, heading for the arches. 'Where are we going?' said Jimmy again. 'Are we going to the Park?'

'No,' said Ben.

'Gloria said to go to the Park,' said Jimmy, beginning to sniff. 'I *want* to go to the Park!' And he gave Ben a kick with his dangling foot.

'You do that again, and I'll put you down,' said Ben.

'Why aren't we going to the Park?'

'We're going later,' said Ben. 'We're going somewhere else first.'

'Where are we going *now*?'

Ben gritted his teeth. 'If you must know,' he

said, 'we're going to Battersea Dogs' Home.'

'What's that?' said Jimmy. 'What are we going there for?'

'Battersea Dogs' Home?' said Kathy, coming up alongside. She had picked up the ball, and was cradling it in the crook of her arm. 'Where all the lost dogs are? Where . . .' she hesitated for a moment, frightened to say it, 'where you *get* one?'

Ben stole a quick glance at her. He was very nervous himself. Then he nodded, shut his mouth tight, and jogged on with Jimmy.

It took a moment or two for Jimmy to digest this. 'Are we getting a dog?' he suddenly shouted. 'Are we?' Then, as Ben didn't answer, he began to bang on his head, and to jump up and down on his back, 'Are we? Are we? Are we?'

Ben turned, and very deliberately sat him down on the wall again. 'Cut that out!' he said. Kathy put out a hand and took hold of Ben's sleeve silently. She looked at him. Then she said, 'Are we, Ben?'

Ben felt quite helpless. He didn't know what to say. For a moment, he wished he had been able to come on his own, as he'd meant to; he should never have got mixed up with these two, always pestering him with questions and trying to make him answer. He hunched Jimmy on to his back again, and strode off, without speaking. Kathy followed, her ball under her arm, very quiet.

The street was dirty. The dust rose in little circles from the pavement, swirled round, then dropped again. Their eyes pricked in the gritty wind. They walked on and on. So many people with bad legs, so many people walking with sticks; there must be a hospital near here,

thought Ben absently. He was looking out for the gate. Someone had told him it was an easy gate to walk past, so he was walking quite slowly now, afraid he'd already missed it. Then his heart lost a beat. He stopped, letting Jimmy slide from his back.

'Is this it, then?' said Kathy.

They were looking down an alley-way. At the end was a gate. It was painted green and white, with

THE
DOGS' HOME
BATTERSEA

on it in red letters. They had both somehow expected it to be very grand, made of iron, with large spikes at the top. But it was ordinary, like a workman's gate, the kind of gate that leads into a yard.

At the side of it was an office. Ben stood by the office door, and hesitated. 'You can come in, if you like,' he said at last.

But Kathy looked back at him, and he could see she didn't want to come, that she was frightened to come in. So rather than have her refuse, he said sharply, 'No, you'd better stay outside. You look after Jimmy.'

Inside the office there was a sort of counter,

and a lady stood there, looking at a large book shaped like a register. She did not look up immediately, and this made Ben more nervous still. He had just decided to go through the other door and get his dog and go out again, when suddenly she said, 'Good afternoon. Can I help you?'

Ben's hand was already on the door-knob. 'I've come to get a dog.'

'Oh. Do you mean you've lost one?'

'No. I've come to get one.'

The lady regarded him.

'How old are you?'

'I'm eleven.'

'I'm afraid we can't let anyone of eleven take a dog. We don't hand over dogs to anyone younger than eighteen. I'm sorry, but you're too young.'

'I'm not too young. Jimmy Sanderford's got a dog and he's younger than me.'

'Yes. But does your father know? Does he know you're getting a dog?'

For a minute, Ben thought of saying 'Yes.'
He hesitated, then said, 'No.'

'Well, will he mind?'

Ben frowned.

'Will he let you keep him?' the lady persisted.

Somehow Ben began to feel this was a slight
on his father. 'It's not my Dad. It's not to do
with Dad. It's Mr Gill,' he said.

16

The lady waited. Ben said nothing more. He'd already said something he didn't mean to. He shouldn't have mentioned Mr Gill. Nothing was going the way he meant it to.

'Well,' said the lady, seeing that Ben wasn't going to explain, 'I'm afraid you are too young. We have to be sure people who take a dog can look after it.'

At this, Ben stopped being worried that he had spoken of Mr Gill. Look after it! Too young to look after it! He, Ben, who had taken out of the library every single book they had about looking after dogs, who knew everything about feeding, and grooming, and training! He, Ben, who wanted a dog more than anything in the world, who had taken a bit of old blanket away from Jimmy – secretly, because it was his going-to-sleep blanket, and he cried terribly till Mum found him one that looked as ragged – so that he should always be ready for his dog! No one could look after a dog better than he!

'I'm not too young!' he shouted. 'You don't

know me! You don't know what you're talking about!'

The lady was startled. But she was unmoved. She opened her book again to show that she was too busy to talk any more. 'I'm sorry, dear,' she said, with a smile that meant 'Please shut the door quietly.'

Ben turned on his heel, and walked out. There were tears in his eyes. Kathy, waiting timidly outside the door, saw them, and said nothing.

He struggled to get control of himself. Then he said, 'I ought to have said I'd lost one. Then they'd have let me take one away. Kathy, you go in. Say you've lost one.'

Kathy backed away a little. 'But I can't say that,' she said. 'You know I haven't lost one.'

'Just say it!' said Ben, furiously. 'You want a dog, don't you? Then *say it*!'

He pushed her inside. She was a dead weight, refusing to go, but he gave her a final shove and she almost fell into the room and against the counter.

The lady looked up from her book, and raised her eyebrows.

Kathy gulped. 'Please,' she said, wriggling and twisting her handkerchief. 'Please, I've lost my dog.' Her voice died away as she spoke, so that the lady had to ask her to say it again, which made it almost unbearable. 'I've lost my dog,' she said with an effort, and tried to keep back the tears.

'What was he like?' said the lady.

What was he like? Kathy's mind refused to move.

The lady looked at her inquiringly, and waited. 'What colour was he?' she said at last, helpfully.

'He was black. No, brown.'

'Brown. And was he a big dog, or a little one?'

'Oh, a little one, ever so little.'

'Just a puppy?'

'No, not exactly ... Yes, just a puppy ...' Kathy was willing to say any words that were put into her mouth. Her own mind would not work at all. Then suddenly she remembered her ball, her 'pretend' dog. 'He comes along beside me all the time,' she said. 'Generally he does, I mean. He never leaves me. He's a very good dog.' Now she really believed she had a dog, and the lady looked rather more impressed.

'When did you lose him?' she said.

'Today,' Kathy told her firmly.

'Well, we haven't had many dogs brought in today, yet.' For a moment Kathy wondered if she should change it to 'yesterday'. But the lady went on, 'Still, we can go and look at all the dogs that have been brought in so far.'

The lady came from behind the counter and took Kathy's hand. They went through a door together – Ben, peering through the crack of the door-jamb, saw them go – and down past rows of enormous cages, all with dogs inside. There was a warm, doggy, toasty smell that Kathy liked, and that made her feel happier.

'These are today's dogs,' said the lady. 'Can you see yours?'

Dogs were standing up against the bars, pink whiskery stomachs pressing on the cage. Dogs were whining at Kathy in funny, high voices. One barked, just once, gruffly, then deliberately walked away from her to the back of the cage.

Next to this cage was a cage full of puppies. They tumbled about and squealed, and pushed each other aside to get nearer to the bars and Kathy. Kathy looked at them all helplessly. She wanted to play with the puppies, and cuddle them through the bars; she would have done that any other day.

Just then, a man came by dragging a heavy sack of biscuits. The lady turned to him, asked him something, and walked alongside him as they talked. She disappeared with him into a little room at the end.

In an instant, Ben, dragging a gasping Jimmy, was by Kathy's side. 'Quick! Get one!' he commanded, dropping down on his knees.

B 4

Kathy was bewildered. 'What do you mean?' she said.

'Get one of the puppies!' he snapped, angry at her slowness. 'I'll put it under my coat. No one'll see! Oh, hurry up!'

She still stared at him, and didn't move. He pushed her away, thrust his arm through the bars, and, straining, made a grab. The puppies moved away. One yelped excitedly. Then another. Soon they were all yelping, their heads on the ground, their tails merrily up in the air, pouncing and growling, thinking this was a wonderful game, and glad someone was playing with them at last.

Ben felt savage. His arm was rasped by the bars; it hurt. He made another grab, and another – and managed to seize a puppy by the tail. He pulled it towards the bars and tried to pull it through, frantically, sure he could hear the lady coming back. The puppy yelped in pain.

'Leave him alone!' shouted Kathy. She

rushed at Ben, hitting him with her fists so that he fell on his back on the stone floor, and she fell on top of him. 'Leave him alone!' she shouted again, tears in her eyes. She heard the door open. She got to her feet and rushed out into the dirty, gritty, windy road.

After a minute or so, Ben came out too, with Jimmy behind him. He didn't look at Kathy. He said nothing. They stood there in silence, the two of them, with nothing to say to each other. Kathy felt sick.

Jimmy said doubtfully, in his special baby voice, 'Want a dog,' and looked at them to see what effect it had. They did not seem to have heard. Then he said, 'Want to go to the Park.' This had more effect.

Ben picked him up, sat him on the wall, and still without a word set off with Jimmy on his back in the direction of the Park. Kathy followed. She was still very shaken.

They trudged on, past the street-sweeper, past the rag-and-bone cart that was standing by

the kerb, past a knot of children who were sitting hunched together on a step playing some game, and round the corner. Kathy sniffed. At last Ben spoke. 'We'll have to get Gloria to go,' he said grimly.

'Gloria?' said Kathy, startled. 'She doesn't want a dog.'

Ben compressed his lips. 'It doesn't matter,' he said.

'But Gloria won't go,' said Kathy. 'She's more busy with Jimmy than with dogs. What's she want to go to the Dogs' Home for?'

'She's *got* to go,' insisted Ben.

Kathy said nothing. Ben felt her doubt, and this bothered him. 'She'll do as I tell her,' he said, and instantly felt himself blushing. They were his father's usual words, but they didn't sound nearly as likely in Ben's mouth. Gloria was the oldest, and it was always they who had to do what Gloria said. Why did he keep behaving so stupidly?

'We'd better get on,' he said huskily. 'She'll be wondering where we are.'

She certainly would. They must be very late indeed. They had left Gloria wiping over the kitchen floor. And after that, she was going to take the washing to the launderette in Jimmy's push-chair, and take it back home again when it was done. And then she was going to meet them in the Park by the paddling pool, with the sandwiches Mum had made for them before she went to do her Sunday turn at work.

She must have been waiting for them *ages*. She wouldn't half be bossy when they turned up, thought Kathy. She certainly wouldn't go to the Dogs' Home.

When they reached the Park, they made

straight for the play-park end, the pool and the hut, the slides and the tree-house. They could already see Gloria by the pond, the battered push-chair that was used for every odd job standing beside her.

Kathy waved rather half-heartedly. But of course Gloria didn't wave back. 'Where've you been?' she demanded, as soon as they were within shouting distance. 'I've been stuck here ages. I thought I told you to come straight here. Where've you been?'

Ben shuffled his feet. Kathy wet her finger and began, very carefully and slowly, to rub at a mark on her shoe. It was Jimmy who spoke. You could never do anything about Jimmy. He was too little.

He said, 'We've been to the Dogs. To the Dogs' House.' Then, his face turning very mournful, 'but we haven't got one.' He shook his head slowly from side to side.

'The Dogs' House?' said Gloria, getting out a handkerchief and wiping Jimmy's nose. 'You

mean the Dogs' Home? What've you been there for?'

She said it quite casually, more interested in Jimmy than in the other two, but the silence made her look up. She saw the tenseness on their faces, and understood at once.

'Oh, you haven't been trying to get a dog, have you? You know we can't have a dog at the flats!' Her voice was impatient, and as weary as a grown-up's.

But Ben broke in on her before she'd finished, trying to blot out what she was saying.

'*You'll* have to go, Gloria! They won't let me have one because I'm not eighteen. But they'll let *you* have one!'

'But I'm not eighteen!' Gloria looked amazed.

'But you can make yourself look like eighteen!' urged Ben. 'With lipstick and high heels, and your hair like Dora Ransom! Honestly, anyone would think you were eighteen – *at least*!'

For a second, Gloria was flattered. Without realizing it, Ben had said something that almost won her round. She considered it. Then she shook it away with a toss of the head. 'Well,' she

said, 'I'm *not* eighteen. And I'm not going to the Dogs' Home. And I don't want a dog.'

'But you won't have to do anything for him,' pleaded Ben. 'I'll look after him. I'll feed him and comb him and take him out –'

'Yes, and where will you keep him?' said Gloria.

'I'll keep him under the bed,' said Ben sturdily. 'No one will know he's there.'

'On top of Dad's bike, and his electric bits, and Mum's hair-drier, and the clothes-horse?' said Gloria. 'Oh, he'll be comfortable on all that, all right.'

She looked at Ben's flinching face and went on, 'And of course, they won't see him when they get anything out. Oh, of course not. He'll be invisible.'

Kathy was lying on the grass. She had shut their argument out of her ears. She put her ball on the grass by her side, and said, in imagination, 'Now sit still, there's a good boy!' She sighed contentedly. She and her 'dog' didn't worry anyone, and no one worried them.

But Ben and Gloria were still arguing. 'You've *got* to go!' Ben was shouting desperately.

'Who's *got* to?' said Gloria in a hard voice. Gloria did not take kindly to an order like that – not from Ben anyway, who was two years younger than she was. 'Who's got to, Mr Clever?'

'Oh please, Gloria, please. I *must* have a dog. Please, Gloria!'

Gloria turned to the pram. In silence she started to unpack their lunch. This was an imitation of Mum. This was what Mum always did when she'd had enough of their arguments and wasn't going to be bothered with it any more. Ben looked uncertain – should he go on? – and then angry. He flung himself down on the grass and scowled.

Kathy took her sandwich, broke off a little bit, and held it out to her ball.

Jimmy took his, stuffed it all in his mouth in one piece, and, eyes popping, grabbed another.

Gloria, with exaggerated grown-upness, her fingers carefully spread out like a dancer's, took one for herself, and nibbled at it daintily, humming a little to show her unconcern.

After a moment, Ben shrugged, and he took one too.

When they had all eaten their sandwiches and drunk their orange squash, Jimmy rushed for

the sand-pit. He took off his socks and shoes, and threw them to Gloria, who said nothing, but merely picked them up and put them in the push-chair. Then he scrabbled in the cool sand with his bare toes, and cheekily laughed at her, and she laughed back. Soon he was working very seriously, making a railway-line in the sand, for a piece of wood that he had found to puff and hoot along. He crawled through the

sand on all fours, making his line. Once he
accidentally dribbled from his mouth, and
looked with interest at the little glass beads of
wet that winked and wobbled on the sand; then
he went back to his work again.

Ben went off to the tree-house. It was early in

the afternoon, and there was no one else there yet. For the moment it was his own private house among the trees. From here, he could see far across the Park. Through the trees the four funnels of the power-station were billowing smoke, like a huge ship on a nearby sea.

Kathy took her ball into a little wigwam

made of branches. Here in the half-light she talked to her ball, and made it bounce up and down, like an excited little dog jumping for a biscuit.

Only Gloria wasn't playing. She looked at Jimmy in the sand-pit. He was very busy, very absorbed. She hesitated a moment, then stood up, and sauntered over to the big slide in a very

grown-up, casual way. She gave one more glance at Jimmy. Then suddenly she dropped her grown-up air, dashed up the stairs as quickly as she could, and came streaming down the slide, free as the wind for two seconds. She shouted out loud for joy. She got to the bottom and stood up again in one movement, and she was just going to run round to the steps for another go, when Jimmy raised his head from the sand. He did not see her where he expected to, and turned round slowly to find her. She could have waved to him, and had her second slide; Jimmy would not have minded; but instead she instantly put on her grown-up air and walked back to him. 'Here I am, Jimmy. Did you think I had gone?'

Up in the tree-house, Ben was surveying the Park. He had caught sight, on the left, of some strange shaggy animal who was galloping through the trees. Ben watched it intently. It looked astonishingly like a bear. But there were no bears in England nowadays, except in the

Zoo. Ben knew that. Had it escaped? Was there a keeper after it? Bears climbed trees, Ben knew that, too – or he thought he did; or was it only koala bears, those funny little ones with the big noses, who climbed trees? Would he be safe up here? If the bear came after him, what would he do? Would he just put out a foot and push the bear down the tree again? Suppose the bear bit his foot off, in one crunch?

All this time, he was watching, and the animal was coming nearer. Now a shiver went down Ben's spine, although here in the tree-house he was sheltered from the wind. It wasn't fear either. He knew what the animal was – and it wasn't a bear. He had seen it in one of those library books.

He climbed down the tree, his heart thumping. He crossed the grass and slowly – for the animal was very large, almost as tall as he was – he advanced on the 'bear', holding out his hand. But the animal danced skittishly like a circus pony, and would not be touched.

Ben decided that was the wrong way. He sat down on the grass. 'Come on then,' he said, patting the ground next to him. And sure enough the huge shaggy creature came and sat down, tongue lolling out, mouth laughing, leaning against Ben like a sack of potatoes.

Kathy came running out of her wigwam and out of the play-park. 'What is it?' she cried. She slowed down as she got nearer, and before she had reached them she sat down on the grass and watched.

Now other children were coming, some from the play-park, some just arriving through the gates. 'What is it?' 'Is it yours?'

To the first question, Ben said, with secret pride, 'It's an Old English Sheepdog, of course, a pedigree one.' He had seen a photograph in a library book. To the second he said nothing, merely sat loftily, not hearing, and left everyone to decide for himself.

After a little while, when the crowd was quite big, he got to his feet and said, 'Come on.' The dog rose and came with him.

The crowd parted hastily, to make way. Some children ran quite a distance and then, seeing nobody had been eaten, came running back.

Kathy stood alone, watching, then quietly skipped towards them and took her place on the other side of the dog. So they walked across the grass, the two of them, as if the dog were their own.

Then Kathy took out her ball and threw it. It

bounced, and the dog seemed to bounce with it. They bounced and bounced, the dog and the ball, and Ben and Kathy shrieked with laughter, and rolled on the grass. The dog ran over and

sat on Ben. Ben spluttered, and pushed him off, and the dog ran round and round a tree.

'How can he see without eyes?' said Kathy.

'Of course he has eyes,' said Ben scornfully. 'His hair grows over them, that's all.'

'I don't like him to be like that,' said Kathy. 'He'll bump into something and frighten himself.' She took a clip from her hair, and walked over to the dog, and he sat down quietly while she fastened his hair back and showed his deep brown steady eyes. 'There, that's better,' she said.

Then they raced in and out of the trees,

dodging, playing hide-and-seek, bumping into one another, shrieking and squealing. The dog bumped into no one; he could dodge better than either of them.

'He doesn't bark,' said Kathy.

'They don't bark,' said Ben. 'Not much, anyway.' He suddenly looked thoughtful. For a moment he was thinking that a dog who didn't often bark was the best kind to have in a flat where you weren't supposed to have dogs at all.

Kathy was sprinkling cut grass over the dog. The dog gave a tremendous shake and shook the whole lot off again. It was such fun playing with the dog at this moment, that Ben shook off his thoughts in just the same way. He could think about getting the dog home later.

Jimmy arrived, gasping. 'What's that?' he said. 'Is it a pussy?' The dog politely turned to look at him, and Jimmy ran, shouting, for several yards, then came back again. 'Is it a pussy?'

'No, it's not a pussy,' said Ben.

Jimmy put his thumb in his mouth, then took it out.

'Is it a bunny?'

'No, it's not a bunny.' Ben rolled over on his back and smiled into the sky. He was enjoying himself.

'It's a bear!' shouted another child.

'It's a lion!' shouted another.

Everyone felt frightened, and some of the little ones ran about in a very small-sized panic. They were not sure whether they were frightened, or pretending to be frightened. Soon they all came back again.

'Is it a baa-lamb?' said Jimmy.

'No,' said Ben, smiling up. 'It's a dog.'

The next second an avalanche seemed to hit him. Jimmy had stood amazed for a moment, then threw himself on Ben, sobbing furiously, and kicking and pummelling in all directions. Ben's smile had vanished instantly.

'What's the matter with *him*?' he shouted, trying to keep Jimmy at arm's length. 'Gloria! Where are you?'

'I'm here,' snapped Gloria, snatching up Jimmy. 'What do you expect him to do, telling him *that*'s a dog!'

'But it *is* a dog!' insisted Ben.

'All right, Mr Clever! How would you like it if you'd just learnt Alsatians are dogs, and poodles are dogs, and boxers are dogs, and terriers are dogs, and now someone tells you *that*'s a dog! Haven't you any more sense! Poor Jimmy,' she crooned, in quite a different voice, 'never mind then. Don't take any notice of silly old Ben.'

Pacified, Jimmy ungratefully struggled out of her arms, and went over to the dog. The dog, apart from giving one very deep bark during the most savage part of Jimmy's attack, had scarcely taken any notice of the quarrel. Jimmy regarded the dog solemnly for a moment, and the dog, from under his hair-grip, looked back steadily at him.

Suddenly Jimmy threw his arms round the dog, and scrambled on to his back. 'Jimmy!' shouted Gloria.

But the dog didn't mind. Waiting a minute,

as if to make sure Jimmy was properly seated, he moved off slowly and gently. Jimmy, his eyes enormous with wonder, his fingers clutching the dog's shaggy coat, sat there tensely, staring down at the dog's broad back, scarcely daring to move his head.

Kathy was the first to recognize that every-

thing was all right. 'It's all right, Jimmy,' she called. 'Have a nice ride.' And Jimmy carefully raised his face, and beamed. 'He's a good dog,' he said. 'My gee-gee dog.'

After that, of course, all the children wanted to ride on the dog. But Ben flatly refused to consider any but the littlest ones. And Jimmy flatly refused to consider even those.

Ben was not at all sure whether it was good for the dog to have children riding him. He didn't worry about Jimmy, because Jimmy was light as a feather; Mum said she thought he was made of plastic. But some of the other children were very solid-looking. So he didn't insist on Jimmy being generous and behaving nicely.

When the dog was tired of having Jimmy on his back, he simply sat down, and Jimmy slid off with a bump.

'Perhaps he always comes to the Park,' said Ben. 'But we've never seen him before. Perhaps he only comes on Sundays.'

'I wouldn't mind just having a Sunday dog,'

said Kathy, putting her arms round the shaggy neck.

'Sunday, Dog Sunday,' said Ben. 'We could call him that.'

'Sunday,' said Jimmy, lying on his back and waving a foot at the dog which he dodged easily. 'My Dog Sunday.'

They played with Sunday all afternoon. Ben

walked up and down with him, saying, 'Heel.' Kathy held up a bit of stale sandwich and wondered if he would beg, but he simply put his paws on her shoulders, and swallowed the sandwich while she fell flat on her back.

Other children stood around, admiringly or fearfully, from time to time; but everyone had accepted now that Sunday belonged to Ben and Kathy, and no one interfered with them or tried to join in their games.

Kathy and Ben were very happy. Their happiness was almost blotting out the memory of that dreadful time by the puppies' cage, and making it all right again.

'I wish the afternoon could go on for ever,' said Kathy suddenly. Ben looked at her, and Kathy blushed. For they both knew that when the afternoon ended, they would have to decide what to do next. If only the joyous afternoon *would* go on for ever. They neither of them said what was in their minds. They pushed the worry away, and went on playing.

But the Park was emptying. Little groups of children, some of them with mothers, were trudging and trailing over the grass, towards the gates and home. Only they and Sunday stayed on.

Gloria was knitting. She was not sharing their worries. When she decided it was time to go,

they would go, and that was that. It was just that it didn't suit her yet.

Ben and Kathy avoided each other's eye. It

was wonderful playing with Sunday. It was
wonderful having a dog. But the afternoon was
coming to an end, and what were they to do
next?

They shouted loudly to Sunday. They ran
further to find sticks to throw. They showed off

more than ever to each other – and indeed there was no one else now to show off to – shouting, 'Look at me! Look at me and Sunday!'

But nothing helped. The sun grew golden and liquid, as it does towards evening, and nothing stopped it moving across the sky.

Jimmy climbed into the pram of his own accord, and curled up, sucking his thumb.

Gloria briskly rolled up her knitting, and stuck it well down behind the pillow. 'Well,' she said, 'you'd better say good-bye to that dog now. We'll have to go home.'

'He's our dog,' said Kathy, scowling.

'He's *my* dog,' said Ben.

Gloria regarded them without a flicker on her face. 'You know you can't have him,' she said. 'You know Terry Barton brought a dog home yesterday, and Mr Gill had it taken away.'

'What – what happened to it?' said Kathy, that worry she had pushed away coming creeping and crawling back to her.

'I don't know what happened to it. He just took it away, that's all. Took it to the Dogs' Home, probably.'

Kathy looked sideways at Ben. Ben's mouth was tight. He had his fingers firm on Sunday's collar. Gloria shrugged and began to push the pram. Ben trudged along. His chin was stuck in the air, but his feet were dragging, and only the warmth of Sunday, the silkiness that lay under the harshness of his hair and warmed Ben's fingers under the collar, gave him any courage at all.

Suddenly his feet caught in the grass, and he fell. At almost the same instant, Sunday raised

his head, looked round and bounded away. When Ben picked himself up, Sunday was far in the distance, and lost behind the trees. 'Sunday!' he shouted.

'Sunday!' called Kathy. 'We're here!'

'You frightened him!' She turned on Ben

accusingly. 'Falling like that! You nearly fell on top of him!'

Ben looked bewildered, and automatically began to brush the leaves and grass from his jersey, his mind trying to deal with this new event.

'Well, it's the best thing that could have happened,' said Gloria. 'You couldn't have kept him anyway. Mr Gill would have made an awful row.'

Ben said nothing. He dug the toe of his plimsoll into the earth, and twisted it round and round.

'He'd only have told us to go,' said Gloria. 'He'd have said we'd have to find somewhere else to live. I can just see Dad doing that – finding somewhere else to live, just because of a dog! Anyway, everyone knows how hard it is to find somewhere to live nowadays, unless you've got pots of money.'

As Gloria was talking, Ben knew that this was the feeling that was inside him too. Inside him

he knew all this, had known it more and more all
through the afternoon. He could never have
kept Sunday. What would he have done when
Mr Gill said Sunday would have to go? Would
he really have said, 'If Sunday goes, then I'm

going too?' And would all his family have said it too, Mum and Dad as well?...

But the other half of him thought, 'My Sunday. Where is he now? Is he looking for me? Why aren't I looking for him?' He wondered at himself. This dog had come to him and said, 'I want to be your dog.' Was he, Ben, just going to walk away and leave him?

Kathy was feeling quite differently from either of them. For Kathy, Dog Sunday was lost. Somewhere Dog Sunday was wildly looking for them, rushing up to this person, rushing up to that person, getting wilder as each person turned out to be the wrong person, rushing about so fast and so wildly that he didn't know where he was going. They must find him! They must stop his wild rushing about, his despair at not finding the people who loved him! Kathy's face was white, and she stared about her.

Ben stopped scuffing his toe, and looked at Gloria. She shrugged. 'He'll find someone else, same as he found you.' He was shocked. She always understood something of what he was thinking, but not what he was *feeling*. How could she think it so unimportant?

'Why don't you just *pretend*? Like Kathy does,' she said. 'Pushing a ball along and just pretending. Why don't you?'

He was amazed. He had no idea Gloria knew what Kathy was always doing. He was for ever being astonished at the things Gloria knew, when he thought she didn't know anything. But now, as usual, she said something dreadful. 'Let's walk fast,' she said, 'or he might find us again.'

Kathy's face clenched in grief and anger. 'I hate you!' she screamed. 'You're a horrible beast! You don't care about Sunday! You don't care about anything!'

Jimmy suddenly woke up. He did not understand what was happening, but he took his cue from Kathy. 'Want Sunday!' he wailed. And he hurled himself out of the push-chair. Gloria grabbed him by the arm firmly, as he hurtled

past. 'Want Sunday!' he wailed again, his face
still red and criss-crossed from the pillow. 'Want
Sunday!'

'Oh, you are *silly*!' scolded Gloria, with one
hand pushing the push-chair faster and faster
over the bumpy grass, and with the other pull-
ing the wailing Jimmy, whose other hand,
trailing, kept grabbing hold of the grass. Ben

followed behind, pale and silent, looking at his shoes. Kathy walked backwards, staring about her.

Suddenly – 'There he is!' shouted Kathy, 'there he is!' She raced across the grass, her hair blowing into her eyes, and catching on her damp cheeks. Ben hesitated a moment, and then followed.

Sunday was standing quietly beside a man and a woman. The man was putting a lead on his collar, and the lady was talking to him in a firm, quiet voice.

Before even Kathy reached them, Jimmy hurtled past. He had broken free from Gloria, who was having trouble managing the push-chair as well, and now he hurled himself on the man, and tugged on the lead, and kicked the man's shins, and screamed, and finally threw himself on the grass and rolled about crying, 'It's *our* dog! It's our Sunday! Leave him alone!'

The man, half-stunned and holding his legs,

stared. The woman stared too. Kathy came
rushing up, and shouted furiously at them.
'Why don't you pick him up?' she stormed.
'Why don't you hold him tight? Can't you see
he's frightened?'

'Frightened?' said the man finally, quite
bewildered. 'Good Lord, is he frightened? He
frightened *me*!' Then, curiously, 'What's he
frightened of?'

'He's frightened of his inside,' flashed Kathy;

and she bent over Jimmy, and spoke lovingly to him.

The man looked dazed. 'She means,' said the woman apologetically, 'that he's very upset, and doesn't know what to do. I know just what she means.'

The man pushed his hand through his hair, so that it stood on end in spikes. Ben said quickly, 'We found him. Is he your dog really?'

'Certainly he's our dog,' said the man.

'They've been looking after him for us, dear,'

said the lady, giving him a special kind of look.

'Oh yes, of course. Thank you very much,' said the man. 'Well, we're going now.' He had not recovered from Jimmy's attack, and he knew his legs would be black and blue for days.

'Have you been playing with him long?' said the lady. 'He loves playing with children. That's always the trouble whenever we bring him near a park. He always runs off to find some children. He left us hours ago, when we were having lunch under the trees. I was beginning to think we would never see him again.'

Abruptly the man said, 'That's a very fine dog, you know! That's a champion!'

'I know he is,' said Ben.

'Oh, do you?'

'Yes. He's an Old English Sheepdog.'

The man was a bit disconcerted. 'Well, you've no right to be taking him like that, you know. Don't you know a dog like that belongs to someone? He's not yours, you know!'

'We didn't take him!' Kathy burst out. 'He

came to us. We didn't take him. He played with us all afternoon, and he enjoyed himself, and he was happy. If he'd been happy with you, he wouldn't have run off like that, would he?' She saw their faces, and relented. 'Well,' she said, 'I suppose he *would* get more fun out of playing with us. I don't suppose you can roll about as much as we can.'

The man cleared his throat.

'Will you come here again?' said Kathy to the lady. 'Will you come here next Sunday?'

'We might,' said the lady. The man, thought Ben, looked as if he jolly well wouldn't.

'We did like playing with him,' said Kathy, shyly. 'We can't have a dog. No one in the flats can.'

'I know all about dogs,' said Ben suddenly, in a loud voice. 'You needn't be afraid we'd hurt him or do anything wrong. I could groom him for you if you like – '

'I had a ride on him,' Jimmy shouted, his face alight with glee as he remembered.

Ben rounded on him. 'Shut up!' Why did Jimmy have to say that? It was probably a dreadful thing to have done.

But the lady said, 'Did you? My Martin has a ride on him too, often.'

Gloria had not spoken at all. Now she said flatly, 'It's time for Jimmy to have his supper. And Mum will be home soon. We'll have to go now.'

Ben rumpled Sunday's huge head. Kathy put her arms round Sunday and hugged him, then smiled up at the lady and said, 'See you next week. We'll always find Sunday for you if he gets lost again.'

The man ran his finger round the inside of his collar and said, 'Good-bye, children.'

Gloria was already in front, busily pushing Jimmy home. Ben and Kathy walked quietly across the grass. Then Ben said, 'We couldn't have kept him anyway.'

He looked back for a moment. Still in sight, Sunday was trotting calmly between the man and the woman. From that distance, he looked like a blue-grey mist, a walking cloud. 'Imagine him in our flat!' said Ben. 'He'd never get into the kitchen, even!'

Kathy considered for a minute, then decided to smile. 'He wouldn't half have given Mum a fright, though, if he'd come up behind her quietly, the way he does.' They both shouted with laughter.

Ben gave a run, and a tremendous leap, and caught hold of one of the tyres that hung from the trees, and hung there swinging, kicking and swinging. Kathy ran too, but she was too short to manage it. She ran here and there, gave up, and instead ran for the swings, and sailed up into the air.

'Oh come on, you two!' said Gloria, pushing

the push-chair. Jimmy was fast asleep again, his thumb in his mouth, his other hand holding a bit of tattered blanket against his cheek. He stirred a little as Gloria shouted, and the ball rolled out from under his legs, down from the push-chair, and trickled beneath the wheels. 'Here's your ball, Kathy,' shouted Gloria. But Kathy was up in the blue.

Gloria bent down, picked the ball up, and put it securely behind the pillow.

Some other Young Puffins

THE RAILWAY CAT AND THE HORSE
Phyllis Arkle

Alfie and his friends are very curious to learn that a valuable horse is going to be delivered to their station. Could it be a racehorse, they wonder? They soon find out that it's no ordinary horse, but one that's going to need very special treatment.

THE HODGEHEG
Dick King-Smith

The story of Max, the hedgehog who becomes a hodgeheg, who becomes a hero. The hedgehog family of Number 5A are a happy bunch but they dream of reaching the Park across the road. Unfortunately, a very busy road lies between them and their goal and no one has found a way to cross it in safety. No one, that is, until the determined young Max decides to solve the problem once and for all . . .

HOT HENRIETTA AND NAILBITERS UNITED
Jules and Effin Older

Henrietta is a nailbiter. She eats nails for breakfast, she eats nails for lunch, she eats nails for supper. However hard she tries to stop, she just keeps on nibbling and to make things worse, her brother Hank teases her about her crazy ideas for a cure! Will Henrietta succeed in her attempt to have glamorous nails?

STICK TO IT, CHARLIE

Joy Allen

In these two 'Charlie' adventures, Charlie meets a new friend and finds a new interest – playing the piano. The new friend proves his worth when Charlie and the gang find themselves in a tight spot. As for the piano – well, even football comes second place!

COMPUTER FOR CHARLIE

Joy Allen

In these two adventures, Charlie gets the blame when his dad's computer program is erased and he nearly misses school summer camp! Luckily, the real culprit is found in time and Charlie gets to go – but will he be picked for the County Rovers Team? Find out in this very funny read.

JASON BROWN – FROG

Len Gurd

At first, Jason Brown is so surprised to be offered a wish that he can't think of anything to ask for. Then he remembers the misery of being afraid of water, and all he wants is to be able to swim – to swim as well as the frog who is granting him the wish. His wish comes true, but with startling results – webbed feet and green skin take a bit of getting used to . . .

RADIO RESCUE

John Escott

Mia is enjoying her holiday with her father by the seaside, away from her mother who is always criticizing her for not reading and writing well. But Mia's reading difficulties lead her into all sorts of trouble when she ignores the Danger sign.

MICHAEL AND THE JUMBLE-SALE CAT

Marjorie Newman

Michael lives in the children's home with his best friend Lee and his precious jumble-sale cat. One day Jenny, his social worker, asks if he'd like to live with a new family and Michael is thrown into confusion, but when the day arrives for him to leave the children's home he is both sad and glad. His new family turn out to be very special indeed!

DUMBELLINA

Brough Girling

What could be worse than the thought of moving house, changing school and leaving all your friends behind? When her mum announces they are moving, Rebecca feels totally miserable – until she meets Dumbellina, the iron fairy.